2

D0987900

LYRA'S OXFORD

His Dark Materials by Philip Pullman

NORTHERN LIGHTS

THE SUBTLE KNIFE

THE AMBER SPYGLASS

LYRA'S OXFORD

ONCE UPON A TIME IN THE NORTH

LYRA'S OXFORD

Philip Pullman

Engravings by John Lawrence

DOUBLEDAY

DOUBLEDAY

UK | USA | Canada | Ireland | Australia
India | New Zealand | South Africa

Doubleday is part of the Penguin Random House group of companies
whose addresses can be found at global.penguinrandomhouse.com.

www.penguin.co.uk   www.puffin.co.uk   www.ladybird.co.uk

Penguin
Random House
UK

First published in hardback by David Fickling Books 2003
Paperback edition published by Corgi Books 2007
This hardback edition published by Doubleday 2017

001

Text copyright © Philip Pullman, 2003
Illustrations copyright © John Lawrence, 2003
Design copyright © Trickett & Webb Ltd, 2003

Excerpt from *Once Upon a Time in the North*: text copyright © Philip Pullman, 2008;
illustrations copyright © John Lawrence, 2008

The moral right of the author and illustrator has been asserted

Typeset in 11pt New Baskerville
Printed in Great Britain by Clays Ltd, St Ives plc

A CIP catalogue record for this book is available from the British Library

ISBN: 978-0-857-53557-3

All correspondence to:
Doubleday, Penguin Random House Children's
80 Strand, London WC2R ORL

'… Oxford, where the real and the unreal jostle in the streets; where North Parade is in the south and South Parade is in the north, where Paradise is lost under a pumping station;[1] where the river mists have a solvent and vivifying effect on the stone of the ancient buildings, so that the gargoyles of Magdalen College climb down at night and fight with those from Wykeham, or fish under the bridges, or simply change their expressions overnight; Oxford, where windows open into other worlds …'

Oscar Baedecker, *The Coasts of Bohemia*

[1] The old houses of Paradise Square were demolished in order to make an office block, in fact, not a pumping station. But Baedecker, for all his wayward charm, is a notoriously unreliable guide.

THIS BOOK *contains a story and several other things. The other things might be connected with the story, or they might not; they might be connected to stories that haven't appeared yet. It's not easy to tell.*

It's easy to imagine how they might have turned up, though. The world is full of things like that: old postcards, theatre programmes, leaflets about bomb-proofing your cellar, greetings cards, photograph albums, holiday brochures, instruction booklets for machine tools, maps, catalogues, railway timetables, menu cards from long-gone cruise liners – all kinds of things that once served a real and useful purpose, but have now become cut adrift from the things and the people they relate to.

They might have come from anywhere. They might have come from other worlds. That scribbled-on map, that publisher's catalogue – they might have been put down absent-mindedly in another universe, and been blown by a chance wind through an open window, to find themselves after many adventures on a market-stall in our world.

All these tattered old bits and pieces have a history and a meaning. A group of them together can seem like the traces left by an ionising particle in a bubble chamber: they draw the line of a path taken by something too mysterious to see. That path is a story, of course. What scientists do when they look at the line of bubbles on the screen is work out the story of the particle that made them: what sort of particle it must have been, and what caused it to move in that way, and how long it was likely to continue.

Dr Mary Malone would have been familiar with that sort of story in the course of her search for dark matter. But it might not have occurred to her, for example, when she sent a postcard to an old friend shortly after arriving in Oxford for the first time, that that card itself would trace part of a story that hadn't yet happened when she wrote it. Perhaps some particles move backwards in time; perhaps the future affects the past in some way we don't understand; or perhaps the universe is simply more aware than we are. There are many things we haven't yet learned how to read.

The story in this book is partly about that very process.

Lyra and the Birds

LYRA didn't often climb out of her bedroom window these days. She had a better way on to the roof of Jordan College: the Porter had given her a key that let her on to the roof of the Lodge Tower. He'd let her have it because he was too old to climb the steps and check the stonework and the lead, as was his duty four times a year; so she made a full report to him, and he passed it to the Bursar, and in exchange she was able to get out on to the roof whenever she wanted.

When she lay down on the lead, she was invisible from everywhere except the sky. A little parapet ran all the way around the square roof, and Pantalaimon often draped his pine-marten form over the mock-battlements on the corner facing south, and dozed while Lyra sat below with her back against the sun-drenched stone,

 studying the books she'd brought up with her. Sometimes they'd stop and watch the storks that nested on St Michael's Tower, just across Turl Street. Lyra had a plan to tempt them over to Jordan, and she'd even dragged several planks of wood up to the roof and laboriously nailed them together to make a platform, just as they'd done at St Michael's; but it hadn't worked. The storks were loyal to St Michael's, and that was that.

'They wouldn't stay for long if we kept on coming here, anyway,' said Pantalaimon.

'We could tame them. I bet we could. What do they eat?'

'Fish,' he guessed. 'Frogs.'

He was lying on top of the stone parapet, lazily grooming his red-gold fur. Lyra stood up to lean on the stone beside him, her limbs full of warmth, and gazed out towards the south-east, where a dusty dark-green line of trees rose above the spires and rooftops in the early evening air.

She was waiting for the starlings. That year an extraordinary number of them had come to roost in the Botanic Garden, and every evening they would rise out of the trees like smoke, and swirl and swoop and dart through the skies above the city in their thousands.

'Millions,' Pan said.

'Maybe, easily. I don't know who could ever count them … There they are!'

They didn't seem like individual birds, or even individual dots of black against the blue; it was the flock itself that was the individual. It was like a single piece of cloth, cut in a very complicated way that let it swing through itself and double over and stretch and fold in three dimensions without ever tangling, turning itself inside out and elegantly waving and crossing through and falling and rising and falling again.

'If it was saying something …' said Lyra.

'Like signalling.'

'No one would know, though. No one could ever understand what it meant.'

'Maybe it means nothing. It just is.'

'Everything means something,' Lyra said

severely. 'We just have to find out how to read it.'

Pantalaimon leapt across a gap in the parapet to the stone in the corner, and stood on his hind legs, balancing with his tail and gazing more intently at the vast swirling flock over the far side of the city.

'What does that mean, then?' he said.

She knew exactly what he was referring to. She was watching it too. Something was jarring or snagging at the smoke-like, flag-like, ceaseless motion of the starlings, as if that miraculous multi-dimensional cloth had found itself unable to get rid of a knot.

'They're attacking something,' Lyra said, shading her eyes.

And coming closer. Lyra could hear them now, too: a high-pitched angry mindless shriek. The bird at the centre of the swirling anger was darting to right and left, now speeding upwards, now dropping almost to the rooftops, and when it was no closer than the spire of the University Church, and before they could even see what kind of bird it was, Lyra and Pan found themselves shaking with surprise. For it wasn't a bird, although it was bird-shaped; it was a dæmon. A witch's dæmon.

'Has anyone else seen it? Is anyone looking?' said Lyra.

Pan's black eyes swept every rooftop, every window in sight, while Lyra leaned out and looked up and down the street on one side and then darted to the other three sides to look into Jordan's front quadrangle and along the roof as well. The citizens of Oxford were going about their daily business, and a noise of birds in the sky wasn't interesting enough to disturb them. Just as well: because a dæmon was instantly recognisable as what he was, and to see one without his human would have caused a sensation, if not an outcry of fear and horror.

'Oh, this way, this way!' Lyra said urgently, unwilling to shout, but jumping up and waving both arms; and Pan too was trying to attract the dæmon's attention, leaping from stone to stone, flowing across the gaps and spinning around to leap back again.

The birds were closer now, and Lyra could see the dæmon clearly: a dark bird about the size of a thrush, but with long arched wings and a forked tail. Whatever he'd done to anger the starlings, they were possessed by fear and rage, swooping, stabbing, tearing, trying to batter him out of the air.

'This way! Here, here!' Pan cried, and Lyra flung open the trapdoor to give the dæmon a way of escape.

The noise, now that the starlings were nearly overhead, was deafening, and Lyra thought that people below must be looking up to see this war in the sky. And there were so many birds, as thick as flakes in a blizzard of black snow, that Lyra, her arm across her head, lost sight of the dæmon among them.

But Pan had him. As the dæmon-bird dived low towards the tower, Pan stood up on his hind legs, and then leapt up to gather the dæmon in his paws and roll with him over and over towards the trapdoor, and they fell through clumsily as Lyra struck out with her fists to left and right and then tumbled through after the two dæmons, dragging the trapdoor shut behind her.

She crouched on the steps just beneath it, listening to the shrieks and screams outside rapidly lose their urgency. With their provocation out of sight, the starlings soon forgot that they were provoked.

'What now?' whispered Pan, just below her.

These wooden steps led up from a narrow landing, and were closed by a door at the bottom of the flight. Another door on the landing led to the rooms of young Dr Polstead, who was one of the few Scholars capable of climbing all the way up the tower several times a day. Being young, he had all his faculties in working order, and Lyra was sure he must have heard her tumble through and bang the trapdoor shut.

She put her finger to her lips. Pantalaimon, staring up in the near-dark, saw and turned his head to listen. There was a faint patch of a lighter colour on the step next to him, and as Lyra's eyes adjusted she made out the shape of the dæmon and the V-shaped patch of white feathers on his rump.

Silence. Lyra whispered down:

'Sir, we must keep you hidden. I have a canvas bag – if that would be all right – I could carry you to our room …'

'Yes,' came the answering whisper from below.

Lyra pressed her ear to the trapdoor, and, hearing no more tumult, opened it carefully and then darted out to retrieve her bag and the books she'd been studying. The starlings had left evidence of their last meals on the covers of both books, and Lyra made a face as she thought about explaining it to the Librarian of St Sophia's. She picked the books up gingerly and took them and the bag down through the trapdoor, to hear Pan whispering, 'Sssh …'

Voices beyond the lower door: two men leaving Dr Polstead's room. Visitors – the university term hadn't begun, and he wouldn't be holding tutorials yet.

Lyra held open her bag. The strange dæmon hesitated. He was a witch's dæmon, and he was used to the wide Arctic skies. The narrow canvas darkness was frightening to him.

'Sir, it will only be for five minutes,' she whispered. 'We can't let anyone else see you.'

'You are Lyra Silvertongue?'

'Yes, I am.'

'Very well,' he said, and delicately stepped into the bag that Lyra held open for him.

She picked it up carefully, waiting for the visitors' voices to recede down the stairs. When they'd gone, she stepped over Pan and opened the door quietly. Pan flowed through like dark water, and Lyra set the bag gently over her shoulder and followed, shutting the door behind her.

'Lyra? What's going on?'

The voice from the doorway behind her made her heart leap. Pan, a step ahead, hissed quietly.

'Dr Polstead,' she said, turning. 'Did you hear the birds?'

'Was that what it was? I heard a lot of banging,' he said.

He was stout, ginger-haired, affable; more inclined to be friendly to Lyra than she was to return the feeling. But she was always polite.

'I don't know what was the matter with them. Starlings, from over Magdalen way. They were all going mad. Look!'

She held out her bespattered books. He made a face.

'Better get those cleaned,' he said.

'Well, yes,' she said, 'that's where I was going.'

His dæmon was a cat, as ginger as he was. She purred a greeting from the doorway, and Pan acknowledged her courteously and moved away.

Lyra lived at St Sophia's in term time, but her room in the back quad at Jordan was always there when she wanted to use it. The clock was striking half-past six as she hurried there with her living burden – who was much lighter than her own dæmon, as she intended to tell Pantalaimon later.

As soon as the door had closed behind them, she set down the bag on her desk and let the dæmon out. He was frightened, and not only of the dark.

'I had to keep you out of sight –' she began.

'I understand. Lyra Silvertongue, you must guide me to a house in this city – I can't find the house, I don't know cities –'

'Stop,' she said, 'slow down, wait. What is your name, and your witch's name?'

'I am Ragi. She is Yelena Pazhets. She sent me – I must find a man who –'

'Please,' Lyra said, 'please don't speak so loudly. I'm safe here – this is my home – but people are curious – if they hear another dæmon's voice in here, it would be hard to explain, and then you would be in danger.'

The dæmon fluttered anxiously to the window-sill, and then to the back of Lyra's chair, and then back to the table.

'Yes,' he said. 'I must go to a man in this city. Your name is known to us – we heard that you could help. I am frightened this far south, and under a roof.'

'If I can help, I will. Who is this man? Do you know where he lives?'

'His name is Sebastian Makepeace. He lives in Jericho.'

'Just Jericho? That's all the address you have?'

The dæmon looked bewildered. Lyra didn't press him; to a witch of the far north, a settlement of more than four or five families was almost unimaginably vast and crowded.

'All right,' she said, 'I'll try and find him. But –'

'Now! It's urgent!'

'No. Not now. Tonight, after dark. Can you stay here comfortably? Or would you rather come with us to … to my school, which is where I should be now?'

He flew from the table to the open window and perched on the sill for a moment, and then flew out altogether and circled in the air above the quadrangle. Pantalaimon leapt on to the windowsill to watch for him while Lyra searched through the untidy bookshelves for a map of the city.

'Has he gone?' she said over her shoulder.

'He's coming back.'

The dæmon flew in and beat his wings inwards to slow down and perch on the back of the chair.

'Danger outside and suffocation within,' he said unhappily.

Lyra found the map and turned around.

'Sir,' she said, 'who was it who told you my name?'

'A witch from Lake Enara. She said Serafina Pekkala's clan had a good friend in Oxford. Our clan is allied to hers through the birch-oath.'

'And where is Yelena Pazhets, your witch?'

'She's lying sick beyond the Urals, in our homeland.'

Lyra could feel Pan teeming with questions, and she half-closed her eyes in a flicker that she knew he'd see: don't. Wait. Hush.

'It would be too painful for you to hide in my bag till nightfall,' she said, 'so this is what we'll do. I'll leave this window open for you and you can shelter in here, and fly out whenever you need to. I shall come back at … Can you read the

15

time in our fashion?'

'Yes. We learned at Trollesund.'

'You can see the clock over the hall from here. At half-past eight I shall be in the street outside the tower where you found us. Fly down and meet us there, and we'll take you to Mr Makepeace.'

'Yes – yes. Thank you.'

They shut the door and hurried down. What she'd said a minute before was true: she should be in school, for dinner at seven was compulsory for all the pupils, and it was already twenty minutes to.

But on the way through the lodge she was struck by a thought, and said to the Porter:

'Mr Shuter, have you got an Oxford directory?'

'Trade, or residential, Miss Lyra?'

'I don't know. Both. One that covers Jericho.'

'What are you looking up?' said the old man, handing her a couple of battered reference books.

The Porter was a friend; he wasn't being nosy.

'Someone called Makepeace,' she said, turning

to the Jericho section of the residential one. 'Is there a firm or a shop called Makepeace that you know of?'

'Not to my knowledge,' he said.

The Porter sat in his small room, and dealt with visitors and enquiries and students through the window that opened into the lodge. Behind him and out of sight was a rack of pigeon-holes for the use of Scholars, and for Lyra too, and as she was running her finger quickly down the list of residents in Jericho she heard a cheery voice from inside.

'Are you after the alchemist, Lyra?'

And Dr Polstead's ginger face leaned out of the Porter's window, beaming at her curiously.

'The alchemist?' she said.

'The only Makepeace I've ever heard of is a chap called Sebastian,' he said, fumbling with some papers. 'Used to be a Scholar of Merton, till he went mad. Don't know how they managed to tell, in that place. He devoted himself to alchemy – in this day and age! Spends his time changing lead into gold, or trying to. You can see him in Bodley, sometimes. Talks to himself –

they have to put him outside, but he goes mildly enough. Dæmon's a black cat. What are you after him for?'

Lyra had found the name: a house in Juxon Street.

'Miss Parker was telling us about when she was a girl,' she said, with a bright, open candour, 'and she said there was a William Makepeace who used to make treacle toffee better than anyone, and I wondered if he was still there somewhere, because I was going to get some for her. I think Miss Parker's the best teacher I ever had,' she went on earnestly, 'and she's so pretty too, she's not just dull like most teachers. Maybe I'll make her some toffee myself …'

There was no such person as Miss Parker, and Dr Polstead had been Lyra's unwilling teacher himself for a difficult six weeks, two or three years before.

'Jolly good idea,' he said. 'Treacle toffee. Mmm.'

'Thank you, Mr Shuter,' said Lyra, and she laid the books on the shelf before darting out into Turl Street, with Pan at her heels, and made for the Parks and St Sophia's.

Fifteen minutes later, breathless, she sat down to dinner in the hall, trying to keep her grubby hands from view. It was the way in that college not to use the high table every day; instead, the Scholars were encouraged to sit among the students, and the teachers and older pupils from the school, of whom Lyra was one, did the same. It was a point of good manners not to sit with a clique of the same friends all the time, and it meant that conversation at dinner had to be open and general rather than close and gossipy.

Tonight Lyra found herself sitting between an elderly Scholar, a historian called Miss Greenwood, and a girl at the head of the school, four years older than Lyra was. As they ate their minced lamb and boiled potatoes, Lyra said:

'Miss Greenwood, when did they stop doing alchemy?'

'They? Which they, Lyra?'

'The people who ... I suppose the people who think about things. It used to be part of experimental theology, didn't it?'

'That's right. And in fact the alchemists made many discoveries, about the action of acids and so on. But they had a basic idea about the universe that didn't hold up, and when a better one came along, the structure that kept their ideas in place just fell apart. The people who think about things, as you call them, discovered that chemistry had a stronger and more coherent conceptual framework. It explained things, you see, more fully, more accurately.'

'But when?'

'I don't think there've been any serious alchemists for two hundred and fifty years. Apart from the famous Oxford alchemist.'

'Who was that?'

'I forget his name. Irony – why do I say that? ... He's still alive – an eccentric ex-scholar. You find people like that on the fringes of scholarship – genuinely brilliant, sometimes – but cracked, you know, possessed by some crazy idea that has no basis in reality, but which seems to them to hold the key to understanding the whole cosmos. I've seen it more than once – tragic, really.'

Miss Greenwood's dæmon, a marmoset, said from the back of her chair:

'Makepeace. That was his name.'

'Of course! I knew it was ironic.'

'Why?' said Lyra.

'Because he was said to be very violent. There was a court case – manslaughter, I think – he got off, as far as I remember. Years ago. But I mustn't gossip.'

'Lyra,' said the girl on her left, 'would you like to come to the Musical Society this evening? There's a recital by Michael Coke – you know, the flautist …'

Lyra didn't know. 'Oh, Ruth, I wish I could,' she said. 'But I'm so behind with my Latin – I really must do some work.'

The older girl nodded glumly. Small audience expected, thought Lyra, and felt sorry; but there was nothing for it.

At half-past eight she and Pan moved out of the shadow of the Radcliffe Camera's great dome and slipped into the narrow alley, overhung with chestnut trees, that separated Jordan College from Brasenose. It wasn't hard to get

out of St Sophia's
School, but those
girls who did were
severely punished,
and Lyra had no
wish to get caught.
But she was wearing
dark clothes and
she could run fast,
and she and Pan,
with their witch-like
power of separation,
had managed to mislead pursuers before now.

They looked both ways where the alley
opened into Turl Street, but there were only
three or four people in sight. Before they could
step out under the gas light, there was a rush of
wings, and the dæmon-bird flew down to perch
on the tall wooden bollard that closed the alley
to traffic.

'Now,' said Lyra, 'I can take you to the house,
but then I must go straight back. It'll take about
fifteen minutes. I'll walk ahead – you watch and
fly after me.'

She made to move away, but the dæmon-bird fluttered up and back, and said with great agitation, 'No – no – you must make sure it's him – please, wait and see him, make sure!'

'Well, we could knock on the door, I suppose,' said Lyra.

'No – you must come in the house with me and make sure – it's important!'

She felt a little quiver from Pan, and stroked him: hush. They turned into Broad Street and then up past the little oratory of St Ann Magdalen, where the Cornmarket met the wide tree-lined avenue of St Giles'. This was the busiest and best-lit part of their journey, and Lyra would have liked to turn left into the maze of little back streets that reached all the way to the alchemist's house; but she and Pan agreed silently that it would be better to stay in St Giles', where the dæmon-bird would have to keep a little distance from them, so that they could talk quietly without his hearing.

'We can't make sure it's him, because we don't know him,' Pan said.

'I thought they might have been lovers, him

and the witch. But I don't know what a witch would see in a fusty old alchemist ... though maybe if he was a manslaughterer?'

'I never heard of that birch-oath, either.'

'That doesn't mean there isn't one. There's a lot of witch-stuff we'll never know.'

They were going past the Grey Friars' Oratory, and through the window there came the sound of a choir singing the responses to an evening rite.

Lyra said quietly, 'Where is he now?'

'In one of the trees further back. Not close.'

'Pan, I don't know if we should –'

There was a hasty clap of wings, and the dæmon-bird skimmed over their heads to land on the low branch of a plane tree just ahead of them. Someone coming out of the little lane to the left gave a startled exclamation and then passed on.

Lyra slowed down and looked into the window of the bookshop on the corner. Pan sprang to her shoulder and whispered, 'Why are we suspicious?'

'I don't know. But we are.'

'It's the alchemy.'

'Would we be less suspicious if he was an ordinary Scholar?'

'Yes. Alchemy's nonsense.'

'But that's a problem for the witch, not for us –'

Behind them the dæmon in the tree uttered a soft rattling sort of cry, followed by a quiet 'Wheee-cha!' The kind of bird he was, the real bird, would make a cry like that. It sounded like a warning. Lyra and Pan understood: he meant move on, we must hurry, we can't stand around. But it had the effect of arousing some pigeons roosting in the tree-tops. They awoke at once and flew down with a clatter of wings, furious, and chased away the dæmon, who darted out into the broad space of St Giles' and shot up high into the night sky. The pigeons gave chase, but not for long; they were less aggressive than the starlings, or else they were simply sleepier. With a lot of grumbling and fussing, they flapped back up to their nest and went to sleep.

'Where did he go?' said Lyra, scanning the sky above St John's College.

'There he is …'

A darker speck than the sky was roving uncertainly back and forth, and then he found them and skimmed low to perch on a windowsill that was barred with an iron grille. Lyra moved towards it casually, and when they were close enough for Pan to do it without alarming the dæmon-bird, he sprang up to the grille beside him. Lyra loved the way he did that: one fluent movement, utterly silent, his balance perfect.

'Is it far now?' said the dæmon shakily.

'Not far,' said Pantalaimon. 'But you haven't told us the whole truth. What are you afraid of?'

The dæmon-bird tried to fly away, but found in the same instant that Pan had his tail firmly in the grasp of one strong paw. Wings flapping hard, the dæmon fell awkwardly against the grating, and cried out in the strange rattling cooing sound that had enraged the pigeons – and almost at once fell silent, in case they heard and attacked again. He struggled back up to the perch.

Lyra was standing as close as she could.

'If you don't tell us the truth, we might lead you into trouble,' she said. 'We can tell this is dangerous, whatever it is. Your witch ought to know that. If she was here, she'd make you tell us the truth, or tell it herself. What are you going to this man for?'

'I have to ask for something,' the dæmon said unhappily, with a wild quiver in his voice.

'What? – and you have to tell us.'

'A medicine for my witch. This man can make an elixir …'

'How does she know that?'

'Dr Lanselius has visited him. He knows. He could vouch for it.'

Dr Lanselius was the consul of all the witch-clans at Trollesund, in the far north. Lyra remembered her visit to his house, and the secret she'd overheard – the secret which had had such momentous consequences. She would have trusted Dr Lanselius; but could she trust what someone else claimed on his behalf? And as for an elixir …

'Why does your witch need a human medicine? Haven't the witches got all kinds of remedies of their own?'

'Not for this sickness. It's a new kind. Only the gold elixir can cure it.'

'If she is sick,' said Pan, 'why are you healthy?'

The bird shrank back into the shadow. A middle-aged couple was passing, arm in arm, their dæmons, a mouse and a squirrel, looking back with curious eyes.

'That is the sickness,' came the shaky words from the shadow. 'It is a new kind, from the south. Witches fade and die, and we dæmons don't die with them. I have known three of our clan-sisters fall sick with it, and their dæmons are still alive – alone and cold …'

Pantalaimon gave a little mew of distress and flowed on to Lyra's shoulder. She put her hand up to hold him firmly.

'Why didn't you say?' she said.

'I was ashamed. I thought you would shun me. The birds can sense it – they know I bring sickness. That's why they attack me. All the way I have had to avoid flocks of birds, flying many leagues out of the way …'

The poor thing looked so wretched, huddled there in the cold shadow; and the thought of his witch, waiting in the north in the faint hope that he'd bring back something to heal her, made tears come to Lyra's eyes. Pan had told her she was too soft and too warm-hearted, but it was no good telling her about it. Since she and Will had parted two years before, the slightest thing had the power to move her to pity and distress; it felt as if her heart were bruised for ever.

'Then come on,' she said. 'Let's get to Juxon Street. It's not far now.'

She moved on quickly, with Pan leaping ahead. A dozen troubling thoughts were passing over her mind like cloud-shadows swiftly skimming over a cornfield on a breezy day, but there wasn't time to hold them back and examine them, because already they were turning down Little Clarendon Street, that row of fashionable dress shops and chic cafés, where the gilded youth of Lyra's Oxford passed the time; and then right into Walton Street, with the great classical bulk of the Fell Press on the left. They were in Jericho now.

Juxon Street was one of the little streets of terraced brick houses that ran down to the canal: the homes of labourers, workers at the Press or the Eagle Ironworks behind the street, watermen and their families. Beyond the canal, the open expanse of Port Meadow stretched almost as far as the hills and woods of White Ham, and Lyra could hear the cry of some night bird out on the distant river.

At the corner of the street Pantalaimon waited for Lyra to come close, and leapt to her shoulder again.

'Where is he?' she whispered.

'In the elm tree just back there. He's watching. How far down is the house?'

Lyra looked at the numbers on the doors

be, in the words of the perhaps not geographically well-informed poet Oscar Baedecker, *'the coastline Oxford shares with Bohemia'*.

Juxon-Street runs from the northern end of Walton-Street west-ward towards the Canal. It consists, in the main, of well-preserved terraces of small and respectable houses in brick. There have been dwellings on this spot for at least a thousand years, and it was in a house in this street that Randolph Lucy, in 1668, established his alchemical laboratory.

Lucy and his eagle-dæmon were a familiar sight in the narrow lanes leading down to the river during the latter part of the seventeenth century. Many were the stories of strange sounds and smells emanating from the cellar in which he vainly tried to turn lead into gold. It was said that he kept a dozen or more spirits captive in glass bottles, and that on still nights his neighbours could hear their faint cries.

Lucy died in 1702, the victim, it was said, of a spell laid by a witch whose love he had spurned. His body was found stretched out in front of his furnace, surrounded by the shattered remains of several glass vessels. On the night of his death, all the birds of Oxford shrieked without pause for several hours, *'with a Tumult and Frenzie the like of which no Man had ever heard before.'*

The precise location of Lucy's house and laboratory are unknown.

The Eagle Ironworks, which now stand behind Juxon-Street, bor-dering the canal, have no connection, as far as is known to the present writer, with the metallurgical experiments of this sinister Bohemian of centuries past. The company was founded by the celebrated ironmaster Walter Thrupp in 1812, partly in order to cast the new *'Thunderer'* cannon designed for use in the Baltic Wars by Her Majesty's Navy. **Port Meadow** (see p.17-19), just across the Oxford Canal, was comman-deered for the testing of this fearsome weapon, which caused great distress and not a little suffering to the market-gardeners of Oseney.

However, for many years now, the Eagle Ironworks has been serving the arts of peace. Manhole-covers, iron railings, lamp-posts and the like are cast in their hundreds of thousands, and carried to all parts of the kingdom by the gaily-painted narrow boats that unload their ore and côal, and take on the finished products, at the busy wharves behind the foundries.

A tour of the Ironworks, with a historical introduction, may be arranged by appointment. Visitors may also see the small museum, which contains one of the original *'Thunderer'* cannons on which the company's fortune was founded.

The Oxford Canal connects the city of Oxford with the great network of canals extending from the Gyptian fastness of Eastern Anglia to the coal-grounds of the West Midlands. For some hundreds of years the canal, and those who lived and worked on it, were regarded with some suspicion by the respectable citizens of Oxford, who nevertheless depended on the canal-boats for the goods and raw materials they brought to the city's shops, markets and factories.

The canal itself is of ancient construction, dating back as far as Roman times. Indeed, a Roman canal-boat was discovered deep under the mud at Isis Lock, and raised by archaeologists, who believe that it was sunk deliberately as a sacrifice to the water-god Fluvius. The skeletons of five children were found in the hold. The boat and all its contents may be seen at the **City Museum** in St Aldate's (p.28).

In the Cold Ages the canal fell into disrepair, and its frozen surface was used as a ski-road by raiding parties of northern barbarians. In 1005 there was a great battle at **Wolvercote** (then known as Ulfgarcote), on the northern edge of Port Meadow, between a raiding party from the Viking kingdom of Jorvik and a band of stout-hearted Oxford citizens, together with their valiant Gyptian allies, at which the raiders were routed and their power broken for good.

This marked the first association between Oxford and the Gyptians. It has continued for nearly a thousand years of unbroken commerce and somewhat wary friendship. The great event in the Gyptian calendar is the annual **Horse Fair** in the second full week of July, during which Port Meadow is bright with flags, banners, tents, and pavilions, and the coloured silks and rosettes of the horses being shown and traded, while the canal itself is crowded from Folly Bridge to Wolvercote with narrow boats from every part of the kingdom. It is said that more small objects vanish from unguarded windowsills during the week of the Horse Fair than at any other time of year; and it is a remarkable fact that more children are born in Oxford in April than in any other month.

Jericho is also home to the world-famous **Fell Press**, in its grand neo-classical buildings in Great Clarendon Street. This dates from the very beginnings of printing in Oxford, when Joachim Fell, a refugee from the religious persecutions in Mainz, arrived in Oxford with some of the types from Gutenberg's famous press. The whole history of Oxford as a centre of printing and publishing is well told in R. Heapy's *Five Centuries of Printing in Oxford* (Fell Press, 20 guineas).

It is said that the buildings of the Press were erected on the foundations of a Roman temple of Mithras, and that the early printers were greatly troubled by night-ghasts. In the early seventeenth century, one Lolly Parsons, a notorious woman of easy virtue, operated a tavern in the very press itself during the hours of darkness, unknown to the pious owners. It was said to be very popular with the Scholars of Worcester and the gyptian boatmen. A plague-pit on the southern side of the main building was accidentally opened during the course of repairs and extensions in the eighteenth century, and the noxious emanations made the entire district uninhabitable for weeks.

Relations between the Fell Press and the University have been close, but stormy. At one point it was proposed to incorporate the Press as a college, and some elderly or impressionable editors, it is said, never recovered from the disappointment of learning that this was forbidden by ancient statute. Today the Press is a busy commercial and academic publishing house, an ornament to Jericho and to the city as a whole.

The Oratory of St Barnabas the Chymist, the work of Sir Arthur Blomfield, towers over the back-streets of Jericho, and is a familiar landmark visible from as far away as the woods of White Ham. A striking building, it was designed in the Venetian style, and dedicated to the lesser St Barnabas, a saint otherwise little celebrated.

It is said that St Barnabas was an early experimental theologian living in Palmyra during the latter part of the 3rd century. He invented an apparatus for the purification of certain rare essences and fragrant oils, and became perfumer-in-chief to Queen Zenobia. He was beheaded of the nearest houses.

'Must be the other end,' she said. 'Near the canal ...'

The other end of the street, as they approached it, was almost completely dark. The nearest street lamp was some way back; only a faint gleam came from curtained windows, and the gibbous moon was bright enough to throw a shadow on the pavement.

There were no trees in the street, and Lyra hoped that the dæmon-bird could find enough darkness on the rooftops. Pan whispered, 'He's moving along the edge of the roofs, next to the gutter.'

'Look,' said Lyra, 'that's the alchemist's house.'

They were almost at the door – a front door just like all the others, opening on to a minute patch of dusty grass behind a low wall, with one dark curtained window beside it and two more upstairs; but this house had a basement. At the foot of the front wall a dim light leaked out into the untidy, overgrown little patch of garden, and although the glass was too dirty to see much through, Lyra and Pan could see the red flare of an open fire.

Pan leapt down and peered through the glass, keeping to one side so as to be seen as little as possible. The dæmon-bird, at that moment, was directly above on the roof-tiles, and couldn't see the pavement below, so he didn't notice when Pan turned and leapt up to Lyra's shoulder and whispered urgently:

'There's a witch in there! There's a furnace and a lot of instruments, and I think there's a man lying down – maybe dead – and there's a witch …'

Something was wrong. All Lyra's suspicions flared up like a naphtha lamp sprinkled with spirits of wine.

What should they do?

Without hurrying or hesitating, Lyra step- ped off the pavement and made to cross the street, walking towards the last house on the other side as if that had been the destination all the time.

The dæmon-bird on the roof behind them uttered that low strangled rattle, but louder this time, and launched himself down to fly at Lyra's head. She heard and turned, and he flew around her urgently, saying:

'Where? Where are you going? Why are you crossing the street?'

She crouched, making him fly low, and that let Pantalaimon fling himself from her shoulder as she rose again quickly, taking impetus from her movement and leaving a deep scratch in the skin of her shoulder as he did; but their aim was good, and he seized the dæmon-bird in the air, and bore him to the ground in a tangle of squawking, screaming, scratching anger –

– and from the house behind them came a high wild scream: the voice of a witch.

Lyra spun around to face her. Pan had the advantage of weight and power over the other dæmon, but it would be quite different with the witch herself, an adult to Lyra's youth, and one used to fighting and ready to kill, besides. What did it mean? Lyra's mind was whirling. They'd nearly walked into a trap – and now Lyra, weaponless, would have to fight to stay alive. She thought, 'Will – Will – be like Will –'

It was all happening too quickly. The witch hurtled out of the door, half-falling, stumbling, knife in hand, her face contorted and her eyes bulging and fixed on Lyra. The two dæmons were still struggling, snarling, snapping, biting, tearing, and each of their people felt every blow and every scratch. Lyra moved into the centre of the little street, and backed away towards the edge of the canal, thinking that if she could get the witch to charge towards her –

The witch's face was scarcely human any more: it was a mask of madness and hatred, so forceful that Lyra quailed to see it. But she kept the image of Will firm in her mind: what would he do? He'd be still, he'd wait for an opening, he'd make sure of his footing, he'd be perfectly balanced; and she was ready, as the witch rushed at her, to meet her force with all the courage she could summon.

But then the strangest thing happened, in a second or less. There came a dizzying blow to Lyra's head, and she staggered aside as a vast white shape hurtled past from behind her, straight at the witch. The air was filled with a

monstrous rapid creaking
of gigantic wingbeats
– and then before
she could catch
her balance,
the witch was
smashed back
and down against the
road by the full force of a
swan, flying full tilt.

Pan cried out, for the dæmon-
bird was loose and twitching in his
grasp. The witch, still just alive, was crawling
towards Lyra, crawling like a broken lizard, and
there were sparks around her – real sparks – as
her knife grated on the stone. Beyond her, the
swan lay stunned, his great wings spread out
helplessly. Lyra was too sick and dizzy from the
blow to do more than push herself up feebly
and try to marshal her thoughts – but then Pan
said shakily:

'He's dead. They're dead, Lyra.'

The witch's eyes still bulged and glared,
fixed on Lyra, and the muscles of her arms still

held her top half rigidly up from the ground; but her back was broken, and there was no life in her expression. Suddenly the muscles gave way, and she flopped to the ground like a rag.

The swan was moving – hauling himself along, unable to stand; and just above, Lyra heard that powerful creak once more, and felt the rush of air, as three more swans flew across the canal and low along the street, over their stricken brother. People in the houses nearby must have heard all this – there must be faces at the windows, doors opening – but Lyra couldn't be afraid of that. She forced herself to her feet and ran to the fallen swan, who was beating his wings awkwardly and scrabbling for purchase on the smooth road.

Ignoring her fear of the stabbing beak, she knelt down and put her arms under the hefty bulk of him and tried to lift. Oh, it was so awkward, and he was full of fear as well, beating and struggling, but then she found the best angle and he came up cleanly in her arms. Stumbling, clumsy, slow, trying not to step on his trailing, sweeping wings, she carried the swan to the end of the street, where the black water of the canal gleamed beyond the pavement.

Over her head, returning, the other swans came past so low that Lyra felt the snap of feathers in her hair and felt the sound they made in her very bones; and then she was at the edge of the water and she bent down, trembling with the weight of him, and he slid heavily out of her grasp and into the dark water with a splash. After a moment he swung upright, and shook his wings, standing up in the water to beat them hard and wide, and then he sank down again and paddled away. Further along the canal, the other swans skimmed down on to the water one after the other, and swam towards him, faint white patches in the dark.

Lyra felt a hand on her shoulder. She was too shaken already to be further startled; she merely turned, to see a man in his sixties, with a dazed and ravaged face and scarred, sooty hands. His black cat dæmon was close in conversation with Pan, at their feet.

'This way,' he said quietly, 'and you won't be caught up in anyone's curiosity. Now she's dead, the street will begin to wake up.'

He led the way along the canal path to the right, towards the ironworks, and slipped through a narrow gate in the wall. The faint moonlight was enough to show Lyra a passage between the wall and the high brick side of the building. With Pan on her shoulder, whispering, 'It's safe – we're safe with him,' she followed the man along and around a corner into a bleak little courtyard, where he lifted a trapdoor.

'This takes us into my cellar, and then there's a way out farther along. When they find her body there'll be a big fuss. You don't need to be mixed up in that.'

She went down the wooden steps and into a hot, close, sulphurous room lit only by the flames from a great iron furnace in one corner. Benches along each wall were laden with glass beakers and retorts, with crucibles and sets of scales and every kind of apparatus for distilling and condensing and purifying. Everything was thick with dust, and the ceiling was completely black with years of soot.

'You're Mr Makepeace,' Lyra said.

'And you're Lyra Silvertongue.'

He shut the door. Pan was ranging curiously here and there, touching delicately with a nose or a paw, and the black cat calmly leapt up to a chair and licked her paws.

'She was lying,' said Lyra. 'Her dæmon lied to us. Why?'

'Because she wanted to kill you. She wanted to trick you into coming here, and then kill you, and put the blame on me.'

'I thought I could trust witches,' Lyra said, and there was a quiver in her voice that she couldn't prevent. 'I thought …'

'I know. But witches have their own causes and alliances. And some are trustworthy, others are not; why should they be different from us?'

'Yes. I should know that. But why did she want to kill me?'

'I'll tell you. To begin with, we were lovers, she and I, many years ago …'

'I wondered,' Lyra said.

'We had a son, and – you know the way of things among the witches – after his young childhood, he had to leave the north and come to live with me. Well, he grew up, and became a soldier, and he died fighting for Lord Asriel's cause in the late war.'

Lyra's eyes widened.

'His mother blamed me,' Makepeace went on. He was ill, or perhaps he'd been drugged, because he had to hold on to the bench to stay upright, and his deep voice was hoarse and quiet. 'You see, her clan was among those fighting against Asriel, and she thought that in the confusion of battle she might have killed our son herself, because she found his body with one of her own arrows in his heart. She blamed me because I brought him up to cherish the things that Asriel was fighting for, and she blamed you because it was said among the witches that the war was fought over you.'

Lyra shook her head. This was horrible.

'No, no,' she said, 'no, it was nothing to do with me –'

'Oh, it was something to do with you, though you were not to blame. Yelena – the witch – wasn't alone in thinking that. She could have killed you herself, but she wanted to make it seem as if I had done it, and punish me at the same time.'

He stopped to sit down. His face was ashen and his breathing was laboured. Lyra saw a glass and a flask of water, and poured some for him; he took it with a nod of thanks and sipped before going on.

'Her plan was to trick you into coming here and arrange for me to be found drugged beside your body, so that you would be dead and I would be charged with your murder, and disgraced. She took care to induce you to leave a trail, no doubt? People would be able to follow you here?'

Lyra realised, with a little blow to her pride, how simple she'd been. Miss Greenwood and Dr Polstead were not fools; once she was found to be missing, it would take very little time to connect her with the famous Oxford alchemist, and Mr Shuter would remember Jericho and the directory. Oh, how stupid she could be when she was being clever!

She nodded unhappily.

'Don't blame yourself,' said Makepeace. 'She had six hundred years' start on you. As for me, she was unlucky: years of inhaling the fumes in this cellar have given me some immunity to the drug she put in my wine, which is why I managed to wake in time.'

'We nearly fell into her trap,' said Lyra. 'But the swan – where did the swan come from?'

'The swan is a mystery to me.'

'All the birds,' said Pantalaimon, leaping to her shoulder. 'From the beginning! The starlings and then the pigeons – and finally the swan – they were all attacking the dæmon, Lyra –'

'And we tried to save him from them,' she said.

'They were protecting us!' said Pan.

Lyra looked at the alchemist. He nodded.

'But we thought it was just – I don't know – malice,' she said. 'We didn't think it meant anything.'

'Everything has a meaning, if only we could

read it,' he said.

Since that was exactly what she had said to Pan just a few hours before, she could hardly deny it now.

'So what do you think it means?' she said, bewildered.

'It means something about you, and something about the city. You'll find the meaning if you search for it. Now you had better go.'

He stood up painfully, and glanced up at the little window. Lyra could hear excited voices in the street, cries of alarm, someone had found the witch's body.

'You can slip out of the yard at the back of this house,' said Sebastian Makepeace, 'and make your way along beside the ironworks. No one will see you.'

'Thank you,' she said. 'Mr Makepeace, do you really turn lead into gold?'

'No, of course not. No one can do that. But if people think you're foolish enough to try, they don't bother to look at what you're really doing. They leave you in peace.'

'And what are you really doing?'

'Not now. Perhaps another time. You must go.'

He showed them out, and told them how to loosen the gate between the iron-works and the canal path, and then close it again from outside. On the path they could make their way along to Walton Well Road, and from there it was only ten minutes' walk back to the school, and the open pantry window, and their Latin.

'Thank you,' she said to Mr Makepeace. 'I hope you feel better soon.'

'Goodnight, Lyra,' he said.

Five minutes later, in the University Park, Pan said: 'Listen.'

They stopped. Somewhere in the dark trees, a bird was singing.

'A nightingale?' Lyra guessed, but they didn't know for certain.

'Maybe,' Pan said, 'the meaning – you know …'

'Yeah … As if the birds – and the whole city –'

'Protecting us? Could it be that?'

They stood still. Their city lay quietly around them, and the only voice was the bird's, and they couldn't understand what it said.

'Things don't mean things as simply as that,' Lyra said, uncertainly. 'Do they? Not like mensa means table. They mean all kinds of things, mixed up.'

'But it feels like it,' Pan said. 'It feels as if the whole city's looking after us. So what we feel is part of the meaning, isn't it?'

'Yes! It is. It must be. Not the whole of it, and there's a lot more we don't even know is there, probably … Like all those meanings in the alethiometer, the ones we have to go deep down to find. Things you never suspect. But that's part of it, no question.'

The city, their city – *belonging* was one of the meanings of that, and *protection*, and *home*.

Very shortly afterwards, as they climbed in through the pantry window with the loose latch, they found the remains of an apple pie on the marble worktop.

'We must be lucky, Pan,' Lyra said, as they carried it upstairs. 'See, that's another thing it means.'

And before they went to bed, they put the crumbs out on the windowsill, for the birds.

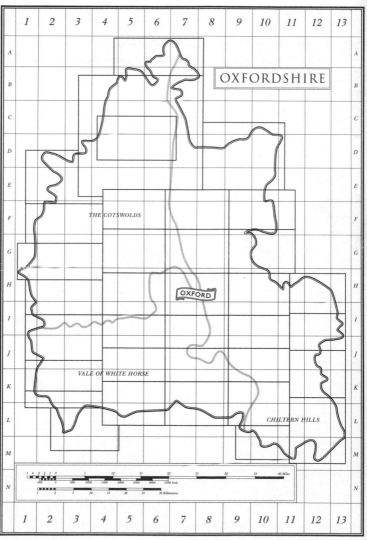

Grid reference labels (rows): A B C D E F G H I J K L M N

Grid reference labels (columns): 1 2 3 4 5 6 7 8 9 10 11 12 13

OXFORDSHIRE

THE COTSWOLDS

OXFORD

VALE OF WHITE HORSE

CHILTERN HILLS

1 4 3 2 1 0   5   10   15   20   25   30   35   40 Miles
1000   0   1000   10000   20000   30000   31000 Yards

5   0   5   10   15   20   25   30 Kilometres

Printed by Smith and Strange Ltd, Globetrotter House, Beaumont Street, Oxford

The 'Globetrotter'

Series of Maps for the Traveller

Smith and Strange Ltd, Globetrotter House, Beaumont Street, Oxford

"The 'Globetrotter' proves itself again and again in the most trying circumstances"
– Captain J.C.R. Freeman, M.C., G.M., Royal Arctic Survey

Drawn with the greatest precision from notes, scientific observations and instrumental readings taken during the most recent and accurate surveys. Noted for their precision of detail and clarity of presentation.

				SINGLE MAPS (Size, 30 by 24 ins.)				DOUBLE MAPS (Size, 40 by 32 ins.)
1. Unmounted	..	..	..	2s. 0d.	..	..	..	5s. 0d.
2. Folded in manila cover	..	..	..	3s. 0d.	..	..	..	5s. 6d.
3. Mounted on linen	..	..	..	5s. 0d.	..	..	..	12s. 6d.
4. Mounted on varnished and rubberised linen, impervious to water and insect damage	..	..	..	7s. 0d.	..	..	..	12s. 0d.

LIST OF MAPS

World in Kremer's projection
World in chromographic projection
World – trade routes
Polar Regions – Arctic
Polar Regions – Antarctic
Brytain and the Isles – political
Brytain and the Isles – physical
England and Wales – railroad and zeppelin routes
Eastern Anglia and the German Ocean
The Hungarian Empire
The German Electorates
The Levant and the Ottoman Empire
Mesopotamia and Babylonia
The Baltic States
Catalonia, Castile and Portugal
The Basque Republic
The Saharan Kingdoms
The Empire of Benin
The Electorate of Zimbabwe
The Kingdom of the Clove Islands
Egypt and the Coptic Kingdoms
New Denmark
New France
Mejico and the Isthmus
Western Europe – political

Western Europe – physical
Denmark and Schleswig-Holstein
Sardinia, Naples, Sicily
The Venetian Republic
Romania, Transylvania, the Magyar Republic
Muscovy – trade routes
Muscovy – political
Central Tartary
Eastern Tartary
Cathay and Manchuria
Corea and Nippon
The Pashalik of Kazakhstan
Oceania
The Austral Empire
Western Siberia
Central Siberia
Eastern Siberia
Nova Zembla and Svalbard
Hudson Bay, Baffin Island, Groenland and the North-West Passage
High Brasil
The Empire of Peru
Patagonia
Van Tieren's Land

"I would not travel without a 'Globetrotter' in my cartridge case"
– Sir Henry Armstrong, F.R.G.S.

A Selection of Catalogues
offering articles of great use to the Traveller

The "Far Horizon"
Catalogue of Camping Equipment,

Tents, Mosquito Nets, Camp Beds, Bathing
Requisites, Canteens, Portable Stoves,
Haversacks, Naphtha Lamps, Hammocks, etc.

The "Excelsior" Cold-
Weather Clothing
Company's General
Catalogue

Furs, Skins, Waterproofs,
etc, including the celebrated
"Blizzard-Proof" range,
endorsed by the Royal
Arctic Society's
Equipment Committee

Northrop's Catalogue

Guns, Rifles,
Revolvers, Automatic
Pistols, Telescopic
Sights, Cartridges,
Swordsticks, Cartridge
Bags, Gunpowder,
Gelignite, Dynamite, etc.

The Catalogue of the Combined
Services' General Stores

H.D. Armitage's Catalogue of Artists'
and Draughtsman's Materials,

including Pencils, Pens,
Pigments, Inks, Oils, Palettes,
our own range of "Girtin" Sable
Brushes, a wide variety of
Papers, Canvas, Sketchbooks,
etc.

Theophrastus Colcroft and Sons'

Catalogue of Scientific
and Surveying
Equipment, including
Sextants, Theodolites,
Compasses, Measuring
Chains, Artificial
Horizons,
Anemometers,
Barometers,
Microscopes,
Celestial and
Terrestrial Telescopes,
Slide Rules, Calculating Circles, Protractors,
Beam Compasses, Proportional Dividers,
and a full range of Photogramic Apparatus

Upchurch and Polk's
Catalogue of Ship's
Chandlery and
Navigational
Equipment

*The above catalogues may be had on application to Smith & Strange,
Globetrotter House, Beaumont Street, Oxford*

BOOKS on travel,
archaeology, and related subjects
published by Smith and Strange, Ltd., Globetrotter House, Beaumont Street, Oxford

By Zeppelin to the Pole
by Lt.-Col. J.C.B. Carborn, G.M.,
O.S., F.R.A.S.

**The Proto-Fisher People
of L'Anse aux Meadows**
by Leonard Broken Arrow,
D.Phil., F.R.A.S.

**A Grammar of the
Finno-Ugrian Languages**
by Arthur Louis Kertesz

**Star-Maps of the
Yenisei Region**
by D.V.Mikuschev

Where the Reindeer Run
by Lars Unsgaard
**Songs and Ballads of
the Lapp Kingdoms**
ed. J. P. Savinen

**With Gun and Rod
in the Hindu Kush**
by Capt. R.T.G. Collins

**A Phrase-Book for the
Levant** incorporating
useful information and
phrases in all the major
languages of the Ottoman
Empire,
ed. James Verity, Ph.D., F.R.G.S.

**A Phrase-Book for
the Nordic Lands**
ed. James Verity, Ph.D., F.R.G.S.

**A Phrase-Book for
the Oceanic Islands**
ed. James Verity, Ph.D., F.R.G.S.

**A Guide for the Traveller in
the Realms of the Witches**
by Karel Powers

The Bronze Clocks of Benin
by Marisa Coulter

**From Novgorod to Cairo:
an Alternative Trade-History**
by Ricardo Pontoppidan

**A Treatise on the
Use of the Sextant**
by Giovanni Battista Kremer

The Lamaseries of Bhutan
by Jasper Wetzel

**Optical Phenomena among
the Glaciers of the Alps**
by T.G. Hammersley

**Some Curious Anomalies
in the Mathematics of
Palladio's Quattro Libri**
by Nicholas Outram

**Polymathestatos: A Festschrift
in honour of Joscelyn Godwin**
ed. by Athanasius Kircher

A Prisoner of the Bears
by Professor Jotham D. Santelia,
D.Phil., F.R.A.S., F.B.A.

**Fraud: an Exposure of
a Scientific Imposture**
by Professor P. Trelawney,
Ph.D., F.R.A.S., F.B.A.

OXFORD ENGLAND

Dear Angela ~ just arrived
in Oxford ~ so strange not
to be 'sister' any more!
I thought you'd like this
postcard ~ such a beautiful
city, and they produce a
card like this! But it does
grow on the place I work in and
a house just around the
corner from my flat ~ That's
something anyway.
Lots of love ~ Mary

Angela Brinson
5 Leonards Road
Lancaster
England

Images of Oxford
Botanic Garden, University Science Buildings,
Hornbeam trees in Sunderland Avenue, Houses in Norham Gardens.

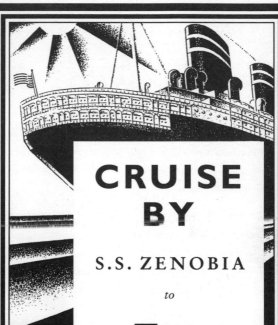

CRUISE
BY

S.S. ZENOBIA

to

THE
LEVANT

A world of romance and sunshine...

OF silks and perfumes, of carpets and sweetmeats, of damascened swords, of the glint of beautiful eyes beneath the star-filled sky...

OF swaying palms and camel trains, of lost and fabled cities 'mid the ever-shifting sands...

OF mysterious souks and bazaars, where the jasmine-laden fragrance of the night drifts out to the plangent melody of flute and guitar...

OF tumbled ruins whispering the secrets of ages past, where the timeless beauty of golden sun on stone recalls deeds of valour and tales of love!

SAIL IN S.S. ZENOBIA, THE MOST UP-TO-DATE AND COMFORTABLE CRUISE LINER AFLOAT, FOR 36 DAYS OF LUXURY, FASCINATION AND WONDER ON THE SEAS WHERE LEGENDS WERE BORN.

Enjoy the delicious cuisine, dance to the romantic music of Carlo Pomerini and his Salon Serenade Orchestra, thrill to the whisper of moonlight on the tranquil waters of the Mediterranean!

An Imperial Orient Levantine Cruise is the gateway to a world of loveliness.

36 DAYS CRUISE BY **S.S. ZENOBIA**
DATES AND ARRIVAL AND DEPARTURE TIMES

	ARRIVAL	DEPARTURE
London		Thursday, April 17, 5 p.m.
Gebraltarik	Monday, April 21, 2 p.m.	Wednesday, April 23, 10 p.m.
Palermo	Saturday, April 26, 8 a.m.	Saturday, April 26, 6 p.m.
Famagusta	Wednesday, April 30, 8 a.m.	Wednesday, April 30, 7 p.m.
Latakia	Friday, May 1, 7 a.m.	Friday, May 1, 6 p.m.
Alexandria	Saturday, May 2, 6 a.m.	Sunday, May 3, midnight
Jaffa	Monday, May 4, 8 a.m.	Monday, May 4, 6 p.m.
Beirut	Tuesday, May 5, 7 a.m.	Tuesday, May 5, midnight
Rhodes	Thursday, May 7, 8 a.m.	Friday, May 8, 6 a.m.
Constantinople ..	Saturday, May 9, 6 p.m.	Sunday, May 10, 6 p.m.
Smyrna	Monday, May 11, 8 a.m.	Monday, May 11, 4 p.m.
Phaleron Bay..	Tuesday, May 12, 8 a.m.	Wednesday, May 13, 6 p.m.
Messina	Friday, May 15, 8 a.m.	Friday, May 15, 6 p.m.
Algiers	Sunday, May 17, noon	Sunday, May 17, 7 p.m.
Palma	Wednesday, May 20, 7 a.m.	Wednesday, May 20, 6 p.m.
Southampton..	Saturday, May 23, 8 a.m.	

Café Antalya, Süleiman Square, 11 a.m.

Excursions available to

Seville	Petra
Palmyra	Aleppo
Antioch	Jerusalem
Athens	Cairo

Cost from 60 guineas.

APPLY TO THE BOOKING OFFICE OF THE IMPERIAL ORIENT SHIPPING LINE, UPPER THAMES STREET, LONDON, AND TO THE FIRM'S ACCREDITED AGENTS THROUGHOUT THE KINGDOM.

READ ON FOR A PREVIEW
OF ANOTHER MAGICAL STORY
FROM THE UNIVERSE OF

PHILIP PULLMAN'S

HIS DARK MATERIALS

ONCE UPON A TIME IN THE NORTH

The battered cargo balloon came in out of a rainstorm over the White Sea, losing height rapidly and swaying in the strong north-west wind as the pilot trimmed the vanes and tried to adjust the gas-valve. The pilot was a lean young man with a large hat, a laconic disposition, and a thin moustache, and at present he was making for the Barents Sea Company Depot, whose location was marked on a torn scrap of paper pinned to the binnacle of the gondola. He could see the depot spread out around the little harbour ahead – a cluster of administrative buildings, a hangar, a warehouse, workshops, gas storage tanks and the associated machinery; it was all approaching fast, and he had to make quick adjustments to everything he could control in order to avoid the hangar roof and make for the open space beyond the warehouse.

The gas-valve was stuck. It needed a wrench, but the only tool to hand was a dirty old revolver, which the pilot hauled from the holster at his waist and used to bang the valve till it loosened all at once, releasing more gas than he really wanted. The balloon sagged and drooped suddenly, and plunged downwards, scattering a group of men clustered around a broken tractor. The gondola smashed into the hard ground, and bounced and dragged behind the emptying balloon across the open space until it finally came to rest only feet away from a gas storage tank.

The pilot gingerly untangled his fingers from the rope he'd been holding on to, worked out which way up he was, shifted the tool box off his legs, wiped the oily water out of his eyes, and hauled himself upright.

'Well, Hester, looks like we're getting the hang of this,' he said. His dæmon, who looked like a small sardonic jackrabbit, flicked her ears as she clambered out of the tangle of tools, cold-weather clothing, broken instruments, and rope. Everything was saturated.

'My feelings are too deep to express, Lee,' she said.

Lee found his hat and emptied the rainwater out of it before settling it on his head. Then he became aware of the audience: the men by the tractor, two workers at the gas plant, one clasping his hands to his head after the near escape, and a shirtsleeved clerk from the administrative building, gaping in the open doorway.

Lee gave them a cheerful wave and turned back to make the balloon safe. He was proud of this balloon. He'd won it in a poker game six months before, in Texas. He was twenty-four, ready for adventure, and happy to go wherever the winds took him. He'd better be, as Hester reminded him; he wasn't going to go anywhere else.

Blown by the winds of chance, then, and very slightly aided by the first half of a tattered book called *The Elements of Aerial Navigation*, which his opponent in the poker game had thrown in free (the second half was missing), he had drifted into the Arctic, stopping wherever he could find work, and eventually landed on this island. Novy Odense looked like a place where there was work to be done, and Lee's pockets were well nigh empty.

He worked for an hour or two to make everything secure and then, assuming the nonchalance proper to a prince of the air, he sauntered over to the administrative building to pay for the storage of the balloon.

'You come here for the oil?' said the clerk behind the counter.

'He came here for flying lessons,' said a man sitting by the stove drinking coffee.

'Oh, yeah,' said the clerk. 'We saw you land. Impressive.'

'What kind of oil would that be?' said Lee.

'Ah,' said the clerk, winking, 'all right, you're kidding. I got it. You heard nothing from me about any oil rush. I could tell you were a roughneck, but I won't say a word. You working for Larsen Manganese?'

'I'm an aeronaut,' said Lee. 'That's why I have a balloon. You going to give me a receipt for that?'

'Here,' said the clerk, stamping it and handing it over.

Lee tucked it into his waistcoat pocket and said, 'What's Larsen Manganese?'

'Big rich mining company. You rich?'

'Does it look like it?'

'No.'

'Well, you got that right,' said Lee. 'Anything else I got to do before I go and spend all my money?'

'Customs,' said the clerk. 'Over by the main gate.'

Lee found the Customs and Revenue office easily enough, and filled in a form under the instructions of a stern young officer.

'I see you have a gun,' the officer said.

'Is that against the law?'

'No. Are you working for Larsen Manganese?'

'I only been here five minutes and already two people asked me that. I never heard of Larsen Manganese before I landed here.'

'Lucky,' said the Customs officer. 'Open your kitbag, please.'

Lee offered it and its meagre contents for inspection. It took about five seconds.

'Thank you, Mr Scoresby,' said the officer. 'It would be a good idea to remember that the only legitimate agency of the law here on Novy Odense is the Office of Customs and Revenue. There is no police force. That means that if anyone transgresses the law, we deal with it, and let me assure you that we do so without hesitation.'

'Glad to hear it,' said Lee. 'Give me a law-abiding place any day.'

He swung his kitbag over his shoulder and set out for the town. It was late spring, and the snow was dirty and the road pitted with potholes. The buildings in the town were mostly of wood, which must have been imported, since few trees grew on the island. The only exceptions he could see were built of some dark stone that gave a dull disapproving air to the town centre: a glum-looking oratory dedicated to St Petronius, a town hall, and a bank. Despite the blustery wind, the town smelt richly of its industrial products: there were refineries for fish oil, seal oil, and rock oil, there was a tannery and a fish-pickling factory, and various effluvia from all of them assailed Lee's nose or stung his eyes as the wind brought their fragrance down the narrow streets.

The most interesting thing was the bears. The first time Lee saw one slouching casually out of an alley he could scarcely believe his eyes. Gigantic, ivory-furred, silent: the creature's expression was impossible to read, but there was no mistaking the immense power in those limbs, those claws, that air of inhuman self-possession. There were more of them further into town, gathered in small groups at street corners, sleeping in alleyways, and occasionally working: pulling a cart, or lifting blocks of stone on a building site.

The townspeople took no notice of them, except to avoid them on the pavement. They didn't look at them either, Lee noticed.

'They want to pretend they're not there,' said Hester.

For the most part, the bears ignored the people, but once or twice Lee saw a glance of sullen anger in a pair of small intense black eyes, or heard a low and quickly suppressed growl as a well-dressed woman stood expectantly waiting to be made way for. But both

bears and people stepped aside when a couple of men in a uniform of maroon came strolling down the centre of the pavement. They wore pistols and carried batons, and Lee supposed them to be Customs men.

All in all, the place was suffused with an air of tension and anxiety.

Lee was hungry, so he chose a cheap-looking bar and ordered vodka and some pickled fish. The place was crowded and the air was rank with smokeleaf, and unless they were unusually excitable in this town, there was something in the nature of a quarrel going on. Voices were raised in the corner of the room, someone was banging his fist on a table, and the bartender was watching closely, paying only just enough attention to his job to refill Lee's glass without being asked.

Lee knew that one sure way to get into trouble of

his own was to enquire too quickly into other people's.
So he didn't give more than a swift glance at the area
where the voices were raised, but he was curious too,
and once he'd made a start on the pickled fish he said
to the bartender:

'What's the discussion about over there?'

'That red-haired bastard van Breda can't set sail
and leave. He's a Dutchman with a ship tied up in the
harbour and they won't release his cargo from the
warehouse. He's been driving everyone mad with his
complaining. If he doesn't shut up soon I'm going to
throw him out.'

'Oh,' said Lee. 'Why won't they release the cargo?'

'I don't know. Probably he hasn't paid the storage
fee. Who cares?'

'Well,' said Lee, 'I guess he does.'

He turned round in a leisurely way and rested his
elbows on the bar behind him. The man with the red
hair was about fifty, stocky and high-coloured, and
when one of the other men at the table tried to put a
hand on his arm he shook it off violently, upsetting a
glass. Seeing what he'd done, the Dutchman put both
hands to his head in a gesture that looked more like
despair than fury. Then he tried placating the man
whose beer he'd spilt, but that went wrong too, and
he banged both fists on the table and shouted through
the hubbub.

'Such a frenzy!' said a voice beside Lee. 'He'll work
himself into a heart attack, wouldn't you say?'

Lee turned to see a thin, hungry-looking man in a

faded black suit that was a little too big for him.

'Could be,' he said.

'Are you a stranger here, sir?'

'Just flew in.'

'An aeronaut! How exciting! Well, things are really looking up in Novy Odense. Stirring times!'

'I hear they've struck oil,' said Lee.

'Indeed. The town is positively palpitating with excitement. *And* there's to be an election for Mayor this very week. There hasn't been so much news in Novy Odense for years and years.'

'An election, eh? And who are the candidates?'

'The incumbent Mayor, who will not win, and a very able candidate called Ivan Dimitrovich Poliakov, who will. He is on the threshold of a great career. He will really put our little town on the map! He will use the mayoralty as the stepping stone to a seat in the Senate at Novgorod, and then, who knows? He will be able to take his anti-bear campaign all the way to the mainland. But you, sir,' he went on, 'what has inspired your visit to Novy Odense?'

'I'm looking for innocent employment. As you say, I'm an aeronaut by profession…'

He noticed the other man's glance, which had strayed to the belt under Lee's coat. In leaning back against the bar, Lee had let the coat fall away to reveal the pistol he kept at his waist, which an hour or two before had done duty as a hammer.

'And a man of war, I see,' said the other.

'Oh no. Every fight I've been in, I tried to run away

from. This is just a matter of personal decoration. Hell, I ain't even sure I know how to fire this, uh, what is it – revolvolator or something…'

'Ah, you're a man of wit as well!'

'Tell me something,' said Lee. 'Just now you mentioned an anti-bear campaign. Now I've just come here through the town, and I couldn't help noticing the bears. That's a curious thing to me, because I never seen creatures like that before. They just free to roam around as they please?'

The thin man picked up his empty glass and elaborately tried to drain it before setting it back down on the bar with a sigh.

'Oh, now let me fill that for you,' said Lee. 'It's warm work explaining things to a stranger. What are you drinking?'

The bartender produced a bottle of expensive cognac, to Lee's resigned amusement and a click of annoyance from Hester's throat.

'Very kind, sir, very kind,' said the thin man, whose butterfly-dæmon opened her resplendent wings once or twice on his shoulder. 'Allow me to introduce myself – Oskar Sigurdsson is my name – poet and journalist. And you, sir?'

'Lee Scoresby, aeronaut for hire.'

They shook hands.

'You were telling me about bears,' prompted Lee, after a look at his own glass, which was nearly empty and would have to remain so.

'Yes, indeed. Worthless vagrants. Bears these days

FINE SPECIAL OLD PALE

COGNAC

70% Proof

0128

MONTJULIEN

SHIPPED AND BOTTLED BY MATTEI BROTHERS, THORSHAVN.
PRODUCT OF FRANCE

are sadly fallen from what they were. Once they had a great culture, you know – brutal, of course, but noble in its own way. One admires the true savage, uncorrupted by softness and ease. Several of our great sagas recount the deeds of the bear-kings. I myself am working – have been for some time – on a poem in the old metres which will tell of the fall of Ragnar Lokisson, the last great king of Svalbard. I would be glad to recite it for you –'

'Nothing I'd like more,' said Lee hastily; 'I'm mighty partial to a good yarn. But maybe another time. Tell me about the bears I saw out in the streets.'

'Vagrants, as I say. Scavengers, drunkards, many of them. Degraded specimens every one. They steal, they drink, they lie and cheat –'

'They lie?'

'You can depend on it.'

'You mean they *speak*?'

'Oh, yes. You didn't know? They used to be fine craftsmen too – skilful workers in metal – but not this generation. All they can manage now is coarse welding, rough work of that kind. The armour they have now is crude, ugly –'

'*Armour?*'

'Not allowed to wear it in town, of course. They make it, you know, a piece at a time, as they grow older. By the time they're fully mature they have the full set. But as I say, it's rough, crude stuff, with none of the finesse of the great period. The fact is that nowadays they're merely parasites, the dregs of a dying race, and it would be better for us all if –'

He never finished his sentence, because at that point the bartender had had enough of the Dutchman's troubles, and came out from behind the bar with a heavy stick in his hand. Warned by the faces around him, the Captain stood up and half turned unsteadily, his face a dull red, his eyes glittering, and spread his hands; but the bartender raised his stick, and was about to bring it down when Lee moved.

He sprang between the two men, seized the Captain's wrists, and said, 'Now, Mr Bartender, you don't need to hit a man when he's drunk; there's a better way to deal with this kind of thing. Come on, Captain, there's fresh air outside. This place is bad for your complexion.'

'What the hell is this to do with you?' the bartender shouted.

'Why, I'm the Captain's guardian angel. You want to put that stick down?'

'I'll put it down on your goddamn head!'

Lee dropped the Captain's wrists and turned to face the bartender squarely.

'You try that, and see what happens next,' he said.

Silence in the bar; no one moved. Even the Captain only blinked and looked blurrily at the tense little stand-off in front of him. Lee was perfectly ready to fight, and the bartender could see it, and after a few moments he lowered the stick and growled sullenly, 'You too. Get out.'

'Just what me and the Captain had in mind,' Lee said. 'Now stand aside.'

He took the Captain's arm and guided the man out through the crowded bar-room. As the door swung shut behind them he heard the bartender call, 'And don't come back.'

The Captain swayed and leaned against the wall, and then blinked again and focused his eyes.

'Who are you?' he said, and then, 'No, I don't care who you are. Go to hell.'

He stumbled away. Lee watched him go, and scratched his head.

'We been here less than an hour,' said Hester, 'and you already got us thrown out of a bar.'

'Yep, another successful day. But damn, Hester, you don't hit a drunk man with a stick.'

'Find a bed, Lee. Keep still. Don't talk to anyone. Think good thoughts. Stay out of trouble.'

'That's a good idea,' said Lee.